THE CHICKEN HOUSE

DISCARDS

By Doreen Cronin
Illustrated by Stephen Gilpin

Ready-to-Read

Simon Spotlight
New York   London   Toronto   Sydney   New Delhi

For Tiki
—D. C.
For Jen and her chicken squad
out the back door
—S. G.

SIMON SPOTLIGHT

An imprint of Simon & Schuster Children's Publishing Division

1230 Avenue of the Americas, New York, New York 10020

This Simon Spotlight edition August 2021

Text copyright © 2021 by Doreen Cronin

Illustrations copyright © 2021 by Stephen Gilpin

SIMON SPOTLIGHT, READY-TO-READ, and colophon are registered trademarks of Simon & Schuster, Inc.

For information about special discounts for bulk purchases, please contact Simon & Schuster Special Sales at 1-866-506-1949 or business@simonandschuster.com.

Manufactured in the United States of America 0721 LAK

10 9 8 7 6 5 4 3 2 1

Library of Congress Cataloging-in-Publication Data

Names: Cronin, Doreen, author. | Gilpin, Stephen, illustrator.

Title: The chicken house / by Doreen Cronin ; illustrated by Stephen Gilpin.

Description: New York : Simon Spotlight, 2021. | Series: Chicken Squad | Audience: Ages 5–7. | Summary: Sugar, Dirt, Sweetie, Poppy, and their mother, Moosh, live in a crowded chicken house until Sugar ventures out and finds a new home with a bathtub, a large bed, and even a massage table.

Identifiers: LCCN 2020036048 | ISBN 9781534487055 (paperback) | ISBN 9781534487062 (hardcover) | ISBN 9781534487079 (eBook)

Subjects: CYAC: Chickens—Fiction. | Dwellings—Fiction. | Dogs—Fiction. | Humorous stories.

Classification: LCC PZ7.C88135 Cf 2021 | DDC [E]—dc23

LC record available at https://lccn.loc.gov/2020036048

This is the Chicken Squad house.

It is a yellow house.
It is a triangle house.
It is a house for chickens.

Sugar lives in the chicken house
with her family.
Her sister Dirt lives in the house.
Dirt likes to sit by the window
and read.

Her sister Sweetie lives in the house.
Sweetie likes to draw on the walls.

Her brother, Poppy, lives in the house.
He likes to rest in a big shoe.
And her mother, Moosh,
lives in the house.
Moosh likes when everyone
in her family is home.

It is crowded in the chicken house.

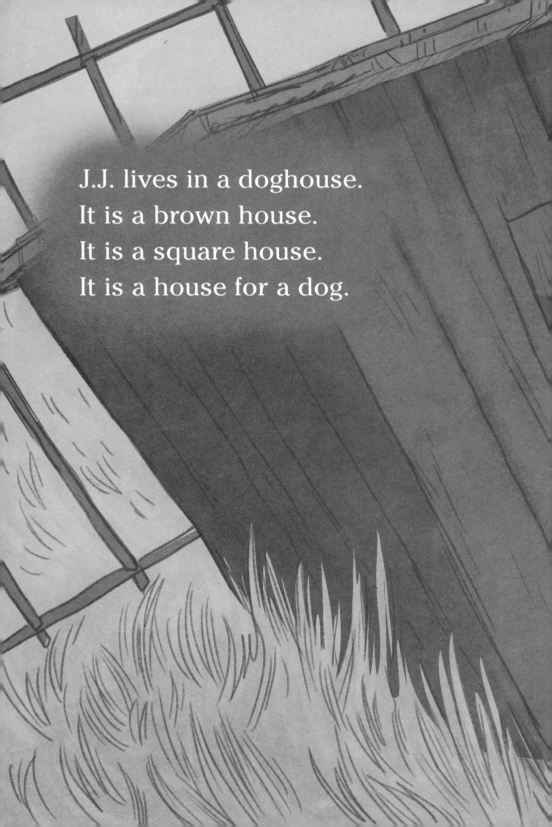

J.J. lives in a doghouse.
It is a brown house.
It is a square house.
It is a house for a dog.

Sugar likes the doghouse better.
It has a bathtub.

It has a big, soft bed.

It even has a table for massages.

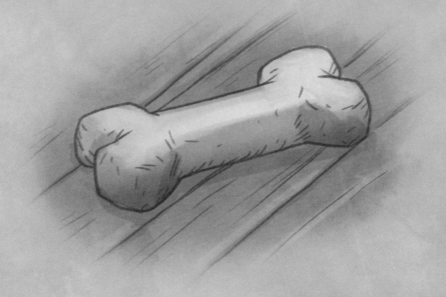

Sugar waits until the coast is clear.

She takes a bath in the tub.
It is very quiet.

She takes a nap in the big, soft bed.
It is very spacious.

She waits for a massage
on the massage table.
There is no massage.
"This is boring," says Sugar.

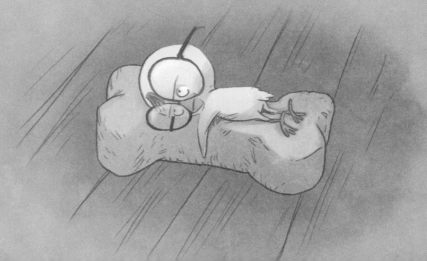

She finds her sister Dirt
reading a book by the window.
"Psst . . . come with me," she says.
"I found a house with a bathtub!"

Sugar and Dirt find their sister,
Sweetie, drawing on the walls.
"Psst . . . come with us!" they say.
"We found a house with clean walls
to draw on!"

Sugar, Dirt, and Sweetie find
their brother, Poppy, resting
in his favorite shoe.

"Psst . . . come with us," they say.
"We found a house with a big, soft bed!"
"Can I bring my shoe?" asks Poppy.
Poppy does not like to go anywhere
without his shoe.
"Of course!" says Sugar.
"There's plenty of room for a shoe!"

The chickens take a bubble bath.
It is not quiet.

The chickens take a nap
in the big, soft bed.
There is plenty of room.

The chickens give one another
massages.
It is very relaxing.

The chicken house is empty.

Moosh cannot find her family.
She asks J.J. for help.

J.J. and Moosh follow a trail
of feathers.

They find a bright blue crayon.

J.J. picks up the scent of an old shoe.

The clues lead to the doghouse.

There are feathers in J.J.'s dog bowl.

There are tiny towels on his chew toy.

There are drawings on his walls.

There is a shoe full of chickens
on his big, soft bed.
They are very relaxed.

J.J. does not like chickens in his doghouse.
He does not like feathers in his water bowl.
He does not like his big, soft bed to smell like old shoe and relaxed chickens.

He does not mind the new picture
on his wall.

Moosh likes
when everyone
in her family is
together.

J.J. lives in a doghouse.

It is a brown house.

It is a square house.

It is a house for a family.